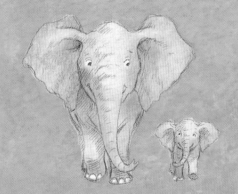

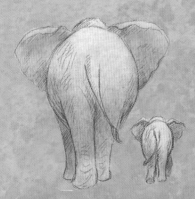

First published 2015 by Parragon Books, Ltd.
Copyright © 2018 Cottage Door Press, LLC
5005 Newport Drive, Rolling Meadows, Illinois 60008
All Rights Reserved

ISBN 978-1-68052-549-6

Parragon Books is an imprint of Cottage Door Press, LLC.
Parragon Books® and the Parragon® logo are
registered trademarks of Cottage Door Press, LLC.

Where you go ...
I go.

PaRragon.

The sun comes up and smiles on us
And starts to warm the early day.

My sleepy eyes can see you move.

Where you go ... I go.

Then out we dash, to leap and play
And scramble in the morning sun.

You push some leaves
aside for me ...

(Hey Mom! Hey, look!
Guess who's a tree?!)

Let's go have fun, and mess about.

When you play ...
I play.

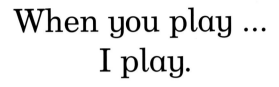

(Oh no!)

The skies turn gray,
It starts to rain,
And you just want to keep me dry ...

(Thanks Mom!)

I run and shelter under you.

Where you are ... I am.

And as we walk on, trunk in trunk,
And talk about the things I'll do ...

(You'll teach me, Mom ...
you always do.)

You tell me just how much you care,

("I love you Mom," I sing to you!)

What you love ... I love.

Then when it's time to scrub me clean,
We'll splish and splosh and splash about.

You wash away my bathtime fears,

(Just don't forget behind my ears!)

When you smile ... I smile.

And when the day has reached its end
And both of us are getting tired,

I'll snuggle up and feel your warmth.

When you sleep ... I sleep.